# Scary Stories

By David Evans

# Table of Contents

## Chapter 1: Origination

Many years ago, there was a large family. The name of the family was the Lectors. They had a young daughter who was sixteen years old.

She was always exploring her surroundings and loved to read fairy tales, before falling asleep at night. Her mother was always so caring; her name was Lucy.

She was a middle-aged women and would often go to the gym and work out for a few hours each day.

The dad was a rather gentle kind of guy who loves to ride his Harley Davidson every day.

His name is Leonard, he’s in his late thirties, and loves to take trips to the local park.

They have a dog whose name is Chase; he is a pit bull mix with Labrador retriever. It sounds like an odd mixer; the dog is kind and loves to be around the family most of the time.

He is always wagging his tail and looking for food, he seems to be hollow inside, but it's a good thing for a dog to have a good appetite.

Caroline had an older brother, his name is Mark, he's twenty-two years old and is always going to parties with his girlfriend Sue.

Sometimes he would come home at eleven thirty at night and wake up everyone in the house because Chase would bark, it would wake everyone up.

Chase was a good dog; he was very protective and always barks when someone is at the front door.

One-time Mark went to a Bon fire party and he and his girlfriend came back home with some burns on their face.

Supposedly the people at the party got really drunk and were throwing wood on top of the fire causing fire and sparks to fly all around.

Mark and Sue were too busy hugging and kissing to notice the sparks coming at them and they both got burned.

Although the burns weren’t that severe they still really hurt. They will have to get checked by their family Dr Mr. Hyme.

Mark and Sue are stubborn and don't like to go to the Drs unless they have a serious health concern. Sue is young and is in her late twenties and likes to do whatever Mark likes to do.

They’re perfect for each other and in a month they are going to get engaged, however Mark didn’t shop around for an engagement ring.

It's hard for him to be separate from Sue because they are such lovers, sues mom and dad are so happy for her.

That the other day they had a party for her and Mark, at the party everyone over consumed alcohol and got drunk and silly.

That was a night they are always going to remember for as long as they live. Their cousin Carrie is a young girl who has been in trouble for most of her life.

She's thirty-five years old and doesn't care about her future. It's been known that she practices witchcraft and has been doing that for many years.

She lives in a one-bedroom apartment an hour or so away from the family, however it's a good thing they live so far from her.

One day the family had got a phone call from Carrie.

Carrie was having a bad nightmare and said that she couldn't sleep, however the family didn't pity her.

She explained that she had a dream that she was at the edge of a cliff about to fall off, a crow flew over and landed on her head.

She said that she woke up screaming and didn't know what to do. Carrie is a loner and never had a boyfriend, although she did try to date while she was attending high school.

She wore thick black make up around her eyes. She considers herself as being gothic, she has long nails that are painted black.

She doesn't like to be seem very often in public; she has always been kind of shy. One time she was walking down the sidewalk to the grocery store.

A strange looking man walked up to her and said to her that she looked familiar that he needed ten dollars for something.

Carrie quickly turned around and cussed at him and punched him right in the face, the man backed away and began to cry.

"Why did you have to punch me?"

"Carrie never answered him and just walked away."

The man walked the other way and never approached her again, he kept on shaking his head and said oh my nose hurts. After that day Carrie hasn't gone out to the grocery store for a week.

Carrie likes to sleep and practice witchcraft. Every Monday her friend Lance comes over and spends an hour or two with her and asks her how everything is going. The family isn't happy with how Carrie acts, so they just ignore her.

But in the end Carrie has caused a lot of bad things to happen to the family. Lucy used to have a cat, that she loved and adored.

The cats name was Falco, she was a large cat that was brown and white and had a pink nose, and she had a long tail.

Falco liked to go outside in the springtime, she would lay down in the driveway and relax, and she liked to chase after the blue birds that would land in the driveway every so often.

Falco knew her name very well and would come when you would call her. Lucy would spoil her and give her cat nip every other day, she would jump all around and be so full of energy. Falco probably weighed like twenty pounds because she was a fat cat.

Her claws were so sharp and would sometimes scratch Lucy when she would pick her up.

Lucy didn't mind this; she loved the cat so much. Some nights Falco would jump up in bed with her and cuddle up right next to her cheek, Falco would purr and quickly fall asleep.

About a year ago Leonard was driving his motorcycle back from work. A young kid that was driving a small compact car lost control and crashed into Leonard. Leonard got thrown off of his bike and landed in a creek.

His left leg was badly bruised and broken in two places, his femur bone was broke in two places. He could barely breath from the bad pain that he was experiencing. The young kid got out of the car and ran over to the creek bank and yelled out.

"Sir are you alright?"

“There was no reply, but then Leonard said I am not doing good, please call 911.”

“What’s your name young man?”

“My name is Robert”

“Do your parents know where you’re going today?”

“Yes,” I told them that I was going to the local video store to pick up a movie to watch for tonight.

## Chapter 2: Bad Luck

I'm so sorry about your motorcycle, I didn't mean it. Okay just make sure that they send out an ambulance, because I am in bad shape and need some assistance.

Twenty minutes later an ambulance showed up, they had a difficult time getting him on the stretcher and out of the creek.

His body was drenched in cold creek water, from the cold water he was shivering so much.

That they were worried he wasn't going to make it, his right hand kept on shaking for a few minutes.

His shaking settled down, for a while and he could relax. Leonard was in the hospital for three weeks, his femur had to be put together.

He was in so much pain and was taking too many pain pills. His motorcycle was ruined, the front forks were bent, the front tire was flat.

Even the frame was bent, the gas tank was leaking. He had good insurance on the bike and was hoping that his deductible would cover the cost for another bike.

While he was in the hospital Lucy would visit him and stay with him for a few hours. Leonard didn’t like to eat the hospital food.

He said he didn’t like that some of the food was microwaved and was mushy. Leonard's favorite meal is steak and potatoes, he doesn’t like to eat his vegetables.

But Lucy always makes sure that he eats his vegetables to stay strong. Mark heard about his accident and came over to the hospital to see how he was doing.

He brought Sue along, she kept on wandering around and said that she was bored. She pulled out her cell phone and began to text.

Mark wasn’t texting he was spending good quality time with Leonard, at one-point Mark turned on the television and Leonard quickly turned it off. He said I don't want to watch a movie or see the news today.

“Why’s that?”

“I’m sleepy and need to rest and not listen to an annoying television set.”

“What’s your girlfriend doing?”

“She is texting her friends.”

That's kind of rude, why don't you have her come over here and at least say hi to me. Okay I will, Mark walked over to Sue. He whispered in her ear, would like it if you came over and said hello to him.

I'll do that then, let me send out this last text and I'll be right over. Sue walked over to the bed and Leonard looked up at her.

"How are you doing young lady?"

"I'm doing good and thank you for asking."

"How are you feeling Leonard?"

"I'm doing alright."

I just get a lot of aches and pains; oh, I understand Leonard.

"Would you take me on a bike ride after you get better?"

"Sure, I will."

Just choose a day, I'll take you for a short ride. Sounds good Leonard. After an hour or so Mark and Sue left the hospital and went home.

Lucy stayed with Leonard for the rest of the afternoon. A week later Leonard was out of the hospital, he even felt good enough to take Sue on a bike ride.

She enjoyed the ride and wanted to go on another bike ride the next day. Everyone was at home, their home phone rang, and Lucy picked up the phone.

Hello, at first she didn't hear anyone. A minute later she heard a little voice, it was Carrie.

Carrie asked Lucy if it would be okay if she would come over and have dinner with them. Lucy said that will be okay.

"What time would be good for you guys?"

"Why don't you come over at three o clock?"

"That sounds fine with me, I'll see you then."

"Do you want me to bring anything along with me like cookies or baked goods?"

"No," thank you.

That afternoon Carrie pulled into the driveway so fast that she ran over Falco by accident, he let out a scream and passed away from getting run over.

Carrie got out of her car and took out her backpack and grabbed her purse. She saw that she had run over the cat, but she didn't yell out a tell anyone that she had run over the family cat. Lucy came to the door and let Carrie in.

"How are you doing today?"

I'm not doing good; your cat was sleeping and didn't see me pull up and I ran him over. You killed my cat.

"How dare you?"

"It was an accident though, okay say hello to everyone and I'll take care of the cat."

I'm so sorry, just get out of my sight Carrie. Once inside she said hi to Leonard and the rest of the family.

Then before dinner was ready, Carrie went down into the basement. She put her backpack down on the couch, she laid her head back and let out a sigh.

The basement was kind of dark, she turned on the lamp and she crossed her arms and took out some items out of her backpack. These items were witchcraft tools that could make a spell against someone. She was just playing around with the items, and she felt a cool breeze blowing past her.

Her friend has given her a jar full of an unknown substance and was warned not to open it. She got a good grip on it and opened it up, suddenly there was a hissing sound.

Carrie wasn't sure where the noise was coming from, she touched the side of the bottle it shocked her, she was thrown down on the floor on her back.

She let out an ouch and said I hope nothing else happens. She went to get back up and tripped over her own left foot and fell over the small table and the jar fell onto the floor and broke into three pieces, a screaming sound came out of the jar. It caused her to fall down again and lay there unconscious.

Her whole body was shaking and the spirit that was in the jar got out and began to swirl around the basement.

The basement door was shut and suddenly all the lights in the basement blew out and now the basement was pitch black

You could hear a pin drop it was so quiet. Lucy came inside and was holding her cat, and Leonard looked at her

"Why are you holding the cat?"

"Because he was killed by Carrie, what?!"

"How did that happen?"

"She didn't see him and ran him over."

Now we are going to have to bury him outside somewhere. A tear ran down her cheek and she wiped it away with her left hand.

"Where did Carrie go?"

"I don't know and right now I don't really care."

I believe that she went into the basement to spend some time alone, maybe you should go check on her.

## Chapter 3: Panic

Then suddenly they heard a whispering that was coming from the basement, so they immediately opened the basement door.

They saw that the basement was all dark and that Carrie was laying on the ground with her face up.

> "What do you think happened to her?"
>
> "Maybe she just slipped and fell, then they saw a shadow coming out of the small closet."

This scared Lucy and she said Leonard I just saw a ghost I think we should get out of the basement; I don't believe in ghosts, but I'll take your word and we can get out of the basement.

Then a ghostly figure was standing right behind them, the figure had a long butcher knife in its hand.

When they saw the figure they both ran up the steps as quick as they could and slammed the door shut. Mark and Sue were looking at Leonard and Lucy.

"What happened down there?"

"You don't want to know"

We might have to leave this house and go to a hotel for the night. There's a killer in the basement and Carrie is still down there.

That night everyone was sleeping and were suddenly awoken to a ghost holding a butcher knife in its left hand.

Everyone ran out of the house and said we are never going back to the house until this killer goes away.

Lucy and Leonard made sure that everyone was in the truck, they took off to the nearby hotel.

Everyone was so scared. So that night everyone was able to go back asleep in peace in the hotel without worrying about the ghost.

The family remained there for almost three weeks, suddenly Carrie woke up and she looked around. The basement was still pitch black; she couldn't see anything.

She tried to walk over to the steps and the ghost chased right behind her and she slipped on the first step and fell backwards and was able to regain her balance.

She ran up the rest of the steps, and quickly opened the basement door and ran out and closed the basement door. But the front door was locked, the dead cat was laying in front of the door.

This made Carrie scream and she ran into the front door busting it open. She ran out to her car and quickly got in it, but it wouldn't start.

She twisted the key and the car started up; she was out of breath from running out of the house.

She drove home and was still so scared that she was shaking and almost had a nervous breakdown.

The house remained abandoned for a while. One day a little boy walked past the house and a cool breeze began to blow around him, he ran off and ran back to his parents who were nearby.

The family was thinking about going back to the house and burning it down, but never did it.

## Part 2

## There's a Zombie in my Cellar

Kirk lived in a small house on the outskirts of a large town, in Maine. Kirk has lived in this small house for most of his life. He has a brother; his name is Wade.

He's a farmer and has a large farm and knows a lot about country living and has taught Kirk how to make his own medicine that helps cure colds. Kirk lives in a big family; he has one brother and no sisters. While his cousin is a real recluse and doesn't like to come out of his house.

His cousins name is Logan, he’s in his late forties and has a good job. He works at the local news company; he doesn’t like change and has set his ways.

So far Logan hasn’t visited, Kirk in five years. Kirk likes it when his family comes together and wishes to see his cousin again soon.

Kirk lives in the middle of the woods; says he wants to always stay in the woods and never wants to move to the city.

Kirks house has a large wrap around porch, he likes to sit out on his porch when it's nice outside. He sits in an old rocking chair that creaks when he rocks back and forth.

His brother Wade has his own beehive and loves the taste of fresh honey from his bees. Kirk hasn't seen his bother Wade, in a week.

Today was a Friday, it was a nice sunny day. It was nine o clock in the morning. Kirk works at the local fish and game office, it's his job to get there before ten o clock each day. He likes to work with the wardens and enjoy being out among nature.

He has a new 2016 pickup truck; it has a nice black leather interior along with heated seats. He loves to listen to country and hard rock music.

He likes to make his radio blare out good country music, today he was feeling more tired than usual. He hadn't slept well that night because there was a bad thunder and lightning storm.

He doesn't like bad storms, because when he was a kid he witnessed his close friend get struck by lightning.

He can't seem to get that memory out of his mind. His close friend died an hour after he was struck by lightning.

His body was chard, he had a bad burn on the top of his head. Kirk is afraid that he is going to be next to be struck by lightning.

Sometimes at night his tosses and turns in bed and can never find the right position. He very rarely has dreams.

Last night he had a dream that there was a zombie hiding in his basement, he could not understand why he had such a horrific dream.

The dream seemed to have dragged on and on, he kept on dreaming. He dreamt that had to look for something in his basement and the zombie came running after him as he was looking for something. The zombie was wearing an old ripped up shirt and he had yellow teeth and kept on growling and groaning at him.

The zombie was missing his left ear and blood was coming out of his mouth. His eyes were all glazed over, blood was running out of his eye.

Kirk was feeling nauseous and at one-point thought that he was going to throw up. The zombie tried to grab him and throw him on the ground, but he grabbed a broom and smacked him in the face with it.

He hit him again with the other end of the broom and knocked out the zombie’s front tooth.

## Chapter 4: The Dream

The zombie let out a moan and tried to jump on top of him again, this time Kirk reached around the gun safe in his basement.

He pulled out a pellet gun and shot the zombie between the eyes with the pellet gun, this didn't do anything to the zombie.

The zombie just came back for another attack, kirk had trouble opening the safe and had forgot the combination for the safe.

The zombie ran at him again, again he kicked the zombie in the head, and he fell to the floor and remained there, and this gave Kirk time to get the safe open.

He just guessed a combination and luckily it opened the safe. He was so happy, he pulled out his 10 mm repeater pistol and waited for the zombie to get up and attack him again. The zombie had great difficulty getting up off of the floor.

Eventually it went after Kirk again, he shot the zombie right between the eyes and it collapsed onto the floor.

A big pool of blood settled around the zombie. Then Kirk happened to wake up.

Once He had awoke he ran out of his bedroom and ran towards the basement but decided to take a detour and go into the kitchen. The dream was still vividly alive in his mind.

The zombie in his dream terrified him so bad, that he pulled out a knife from the knife drawer in the kitchen and held it firmly in his hands.

His palms were becoming sweaty, some sweat was pouring from his forehead, although he was still half asleep.

As he held onto the knife he carefully opened the basement door expecting to see a zombie staring back at him.

His heart was beating fast, he couldn't calm himself down. His arms and legs began to tremble, he continued to sweat a cool sweat.

His eyes were now as big as saucers, he was ready for a zombie to come jumping out. Alright zombie if you're in my basement you better get out or else.

I have a knife, I'm not afraid to use it on you zombie. Now come on zombie come out and fight me, but nothing happened.

Kirk thought to himself well no zombies have appeared yet, maybe there's not a zombie in my basement after all. Kirk kept the basement door open waiting.

But nothing ever happened so he walked over to the basement steps and began to slowly walk down the steep basement steps.

The basement was so dark, that he could not see anything. He reached over by the wall off to his left and found the light switch and flicked it on, all the lights in the basement turned on.

Although the basement wasn't completely redone and had some work to be done to it. The dry wall at the far end of the basement was looking bad and has to be replaced soon.

In the middle of the basement was an old couch and three bar stools. Behind the three bar stools was an old poker table.

He had set this poker table up when he moved into the house. There's a nice Budweiser light hanging over top of the poker table.

The poker table is large and could comfortably seat four people. The poker table was given to Kirk by his best friend over five years ago now.

He stood by the poker table and remembered all the great memories he used to have with all his good buddies.

Kirk loves to play poker and also loves to play pool. He has never had a pool table but in the last month has been checking into buying one.

However, he doesn't know how he is going to get a big heavy pool table down the steep basement steps.

All of his friends are currently away on vacation in Mexico for two months. The poker table had a layer of dust on it.

He took his left hand and wiped the dust off; he had a disgusted look on his face because of all the dust and dirt on his fingers.

He bent down and saw that there was a big cobweb that must have been there for years. There was no spider, he was relieved to know that.

The basement had a bad stinky smell to it though, Kirk just couldn't figure out why, that he had mold growing in his basement.

He had done tests on his basement and couldn't seem to find where the mold was growing. He let out a sneeze and kept on looking through his basement.

He looked under his couch and there was a blow-up doll beneath the couch. Although most of the air was out of it. It must have been sitting there for two years.

Then he walked over towards the right side of his basement and took a look at his gun safe. The safe was securely locked and he did forget the combination as he stood there staring at it.

He thought to himself why I'm so forgetful lately, as he was shaking his head in disgust and anger.

Then he thought on I'm even taking memories pills and still can't remember a thing.

He began to scratch his head and try to think what the combination to his safe was.

He even wrote down the combination and now can't find the very paper he had written it on. The basement felt like it was getting hot, so he turned on the fan.

The fan turned on but moved so slowly like it was going to break, it kept on making an annoying sweeqking noise.

So, he flicked the switch to the fan turning it off, he thought to himself I'm getting tired of things not working around this house.

Then suddenly he heard a loud crashing sound, he wasn't sure what it was. He ran up the basement steps as quickly as he could and looked out his front window.

He saw a large semi-truck that had crashed into a light pole almost right beside his house.

The light pole had fallen onto the top of the truck which caused a power line to also fall down into the street.

There were live wires sticking out all over the place near the truck. Black smoke was bellowing out of the trucks bent hood. One of its rear tires had blown out causing him to lose control and crash.

Kirk was concerned about the driver of the truck and immediately opened the front door and ran out in his front yard.

The semi looked like it was really in bad shape. The live wires were a danger to Kirk and anyone else who might be walking along the street. He could smell the strong smell of gasoline.

There was gas coming out of the semi's gas tank, he couldn't figure out what caused the gas tank to get a hole in it. Gallons of gas had already poured out.

Kirk could see the gas running down the street towards his house. The sky was turning all black and gray and this ment that it was going to rain real soon.

Suddenly a bolt of lightning struck the light pole and causing a fire to start besides where all the gas was.

Kirk was so nervous about the lightening that he stood back and observed the whole situation as it unfolded. He was still very concerned about the driver of the semi.

## Chapter 5: The Scene

He thought the driver must be so scared that he isn't moving and trying to get to safety away from the truck and the fire.

Now the fire was about to engulf the whole back of the semi-truck. Even the tires on the semi were on fire, he was surprised that the fire department didn't show up yet.

He thought to himself there's no reason for me to be standing here if I'm not going to help the stranded semi driver.

Then he thought I'm going to head back inside and see what else I can find in my basement.

He slowly turned away from the horrific crash scene and walked back towards his front door and walked back into his house.

He happened to look behind him and saw that the fire was still going.

Kirk was feeling like he was out of breath, he looked at the clock on the wall in the living room and saw that it was going on 9:43 am.

He thought to himself oh great now I'm going to be late to work, my boss May fire me. He thought oh well hopefully if I get going now, I'll get to work before ten o clock.

He walked over to the top of the steps of the basement and looked down in the basement again.

He thought I'm going to go back down in the basement and finish what I was doing. He didn't realize how quickly the time was passing by. Once again he let out a sneeze and his eyes began to itch from the smell of mold.

He was still so curious about what was going on at the scene of the accident, but he remained down in the basement. He walked over to his gun safe.

He had left the gun safe open; he took out his forty-five-caliber pistol and checked to make sure it was loaded.

The clip of the pistol was full of self-protection rounds, he placed the pistol in his left side pocket.

The gun was so heavy that it fell through his pocket and fell onto the floor. He didn't think that the gun's weight would have caused his pocket to tare.

He bent down and picked up the gun, and with his other hand he closed up the gun safe. He was tired of being in his basement, he turned off the light and headed back upstairs.

He almost tripped over the top step and hit his head when he fell. But he didn't let the gun drop on the floor even though he had fallen.

He slowly got back up and closed the basement door behind him. He let out a moan and walked back the hallway to his bedroom.

He walked over to the sink and washed up his face and hands and this made him feel much better. He was still full of sweat and couldn't stand it.

He thought to himself I don't care if I'm late for work, I'm going to take a shower and then head off to work.

He went to walk over to the shower and there were several stink bugs flying around in his shower. The one stink bug was much larger than the rest of them.

He's not afraid of stink bugs but don't like them in his house. He took a towel from next to the sink and threw it at the three stinks that were buzzing around.

He was able to hit the stinks bugs with the white towel. He bent over and lifted up the towel to see if they were still alive. The three stinks bugs were toes up, but they stank to high heaven, he couldn't stand the smell. He almost threw up his breakfast.

Then he got in the shower and made sure that he washed himself up good. His under arms stank so bad that it made him grimace while he was washing them.

The water was a nice temperature, but quickly turned too cold and made him rush to get out. The cold water bothered him so much that he got out of the shower, right away.

He got out and dried himself off with a towel and quickly walked over to his closet and picked out a nice dress shirt and pants and put them on.

He looked around in his big closet for his nice pair of sneakers, he doesn't like to wear boots or flip flops. He says that the boots make his feet sweat too much while he's at work.

He was feeling refreshed and was no longer sweaty, he lifted up his shirt and put on his deodorant. He was feeling frustrated from everything that he was going through that morning.

He heard his house phone ringing and ran into the living room and picked it up. He answered and it was Wade.

"How are you doing?

"I'm doing good thanks"

"How about you?"

"I'm doing good too"

"Why are you calling?"

"I wanted to invite you to come over to my place tonight and we can have some drinks together."

That sounds good but I won't be back from work, until almost six o clock tonight. That’s okay, I think we need to spend more time together. I agree with that it's always nice to be with you, you as well.

“How's your morning going?”

“It's not going well at all”

“I’m going to be late for work.”

“Why are you going to be late to work?”

“It's a long story I’ll tell you later about it.”

Then I’ll let you go and see you later. Alright that sounds good, bye now. He placed the phone back in its cradle on the coffee table.

He took a moment to tuck in his shirt, he looked at the clock in his living room again and it was going on ten o clock. He thought to himself oh great now I'm going to be late for sure.

He was feeling overwhelmed all of a sudden. He grabbed his keys off the shelf by the front door, he happened to look out his bay window.

He saw a large red fire engine and ladder truck parked in the middle of the street. There was also a big black truck, parked in his driveway, blocking his way out.

This really made him irritated, his nostrils were flaring. He was shaking his head, he thought I'm going to have to go out there and tell him to move his truck so that I can get to work.

As he kept watching the firemen he let out a yawn and thought about how his workday was going to go. He thought on oh well, I hope I still have a good day at work.

There was an ambulance parked in his neighbors front yard, there was no room in the street for it. The ambulance was ready to pull out and head to the hospital.

He thought I hope that truck driver is going to be okay. It was now pouring down raining and this made the situation worse for the firefighters.

He saw that there were three firemen walking around the semi-truck and they were looking at the damage that had happened to the truck and the light pole.

The electrical wires were still exposed, and the firemen didn't seem to know what to do about the exposed wires.

They just walked away and went back to the fire truck. The firefighters were getting wet as they were standing out in the rain.

This kind of irritated them, they all had a frowns on their faces. All of their faces looked rough and unshaven.

## Chapter 6: Activity

Finally, a man came walking over towards, the black truck and got into it. He slammed the driver's side door shut with great attitude.

He was a big heavy man; you could tell that he was angry because his truck was shaking back and forth. Now Kirk could get out of his driveway.

He was glad to see him leave, Kirk slowly got into his Pickup truck. He didn't turn on his radio and put the truck into gear and pulled out of his driveway.

Kirk thought to himself I hope there's not a lot of traffic on the road today. Then he thought since I'm speeding and not doing the speed limit I might get a speeding ticket.

He wasn't trying to think negative, but negativity just came coming to mind. Suddenly he came upon a stop sign and had to slam on the brakes.

Some of the files and papers that he had in his truck fell off the middle console and fell onto the dirty floor of his truck.

He happened to look up and he saw that there was a mother skunk and three of its adorable babies.

The mother didn't even notice the truck and kept on walking over to the other side of the road. One of the three skunk babies didn't keep up with the rest of the babies.

The mother skunk stopped for a moment and looked back at her baby. She remained there for a good five minutes, then disappeared back into the woods.

Kirk put his foot back on the accelerator and pull out and drove on. He was wearing a pair of his sunglasses; they were too dark because it was an overcast day. He placed his sunglasses back in the sunglasses holder above his head.

The sky kept on growing darker by the moment and this was kind of concerning to him.

Suddenly Kirks seat belt came up and tighten, he couldn't get it lose. He stopped the truck and pulled on the seat back to get it to loosen.

But had no such luck, he pushed hard on the button and just took the seat back completely off.

After a minute he tried to put the seat belt back on. This time he got the seat belt on, and it felt just fine.

He drove off again, now there were two cars behind him, he was coming upon a railroad crossing.

There was a train coming so the arms came down and he had to wait behind them while the train passed by.

The train seemed to be moving slower than usual, Kirk thought to himself, oh my goodness, what's going to happen next. It seemed like the train was in slow motion to him, but eventually it passed.

He could pull out and get on the road once more. One of the cars behind him honked his horn at him. Kirk pressed on the accelerator and now was going the speed limit, which was thirty-five miles per hour.

Kirk happened to look down at the gas gauge and it was showing half a tank, he thought to himself maybe I should stop in at the gas station and get some gas and a magazine.

Every time that he does to the gas station he has to buy a hunting magazine and some crackers for a snack.

But today he wasn't feeling hungry for crackers and didn't feel like even walking into the gas station today, he knew that he had to.

After driving another half mile, he came upon a gas station off to his left. There were no other cars at the gas station, there was tall skinny guy with long hair. who was smoking a cigarette and was standing by the door of the station.

When Kirk pulled up the guy quickly ran back into the station. Kirk thought to himself oh boy, here's another hippy working at the station. Kirk doesn't like when people smoke, especially around him.

He carefully pulled up next to a gas pump and turned off his truck. He looked up at the gas prices today, it said that gas was 2:25 per gallon. Then a fly came flying in the open driver's side window.

The fly began to buzz around Kirks head and annoyed him so much that got out of his truck and walked over to the entrance of the station.

The long-haired man was standing directly behind the counter and had a grimace on his face.

"Good day Sir, how are you?"

"I'm doing good today"

"How much gas would you like to put in your truck?"

"I want to put fifty dollars in the tank"

He carefully handed fifty dollars to the man. Thank you Sir, have a good rest of the day.

Kirk walked back to the gas pump and opened the gas cap and began to pour the gas into his truck. Suddenly a motorcycle came cruising on into the station.

The rider had no passenger with him but had an assault rifle strapped to his back and also was wearing a pistol holster.

The rider was wearing an all-black leather jacket and was also wearing black chaps. He turned the bike off and let it rest on its kick stand.

He was wearing big heavy boots and had a tattoo on his neck, on the back of his jacket was some kind of emblem.

Kirk thought to himself maybe he is in a biker gang of some kind. The biker was wearing a big black helmet, he quickly took off the helmet and had a big smile on his face. His face was clean shaven, he took his left hand and brushed it up against his chin and then grimaced.

He looked right over at Kirk then continued on to walk towards the station. Some geese were flying over, the biker took his gun off of his back and aimed it up in the air at the geese.

Then after a minute he placed the gun on his back again and opened the door to the station and walked in.

Kirk saw that the man behind the counter brought his arms almost like he was going to get shot.

A loud bang sound came from the station, and the window that was right behind the station was blown out by the round shot by the biker.

Kirk didn't want to think the worst, but he knew that something wasn't right and that he should probably get out of there before he got shot.

He quickly opened up the door to his truck and climbed in and hit the accelerator so hard that it made the back tires of his truck to spin out. He laid a patch and took off out of there.

He didn't even look back and just kept on going down the road. Then as he was driving along he saw a cop.

He was speeding and not following the speed limit. But didn't seem to care, Kirk looked in his rear-view mirror and now there was nobody behind him. He was glad of this and had one more mile to go before he reached where his work was. The mile passed by quickly and before he knew it.

## Chapter 7: Occupied

He was pulling into the parking lot of where he worked. He got out of his truck and wasn't feeling ready to walk into his office, he knew that he had to.

He opened the door and walked into the office. He walked down the hallway and one of his coworkers passed by him and gave him a dirty look.

"What's the problem?"

"You're late again; you should be fired. I have an explanation for why I'm late."

Don't even try to make me feel bad for you, you know that when you have a job you must show up at it in time.

"Are you really busy today?"

"No," I'm not going to do your job for you, I know that. I'll talk to you later then, bye now.

Kirk got into his office; it was a mess. There were papers all spread out on his big brown wooden desk, his glass of coffee was still sitting there, from yesterday. There was a fly buzzing around his coffee cup.

He watched the fly and took a moment and looked for his fly swatter, as he did that his boss came walking in.

Lewis was a good-looking man with his hair combed back and he was wearing a fine man's suit and was wearing a blue tie.

He was wearing nice black leather dress shoes. He must have had an itch on his head and began to scratch his head.

"What exactly are you doing?"

"I was just looking for something."

"Have you looked at the clock lately?"

"No," I haven't, you're late again today and that's no good.

"What's your excuse this time?"

"I don't have an excuse; I have a good reason."

Go ahead and tell me all about it. There was an accident right out in front of my house, a telephone pole fell into my yard, I couldn't get my truck out of my driveway.

"You aren't off the hook yet, why not?"

"Cameron told me that you were harassing him as you and him walked past each other in the hallway."

"Now is that true, or what?"

"No," it's true, I don't think I harassed him.

That's not what he said, I'm fed up with him.

"Did he say anything else to you?"

"No," that's a good thing, now stop looking for whatever it was you were looking for and get to work or I'll have to fire you.

Now go sit down in your desk chair and get to work. I'll talk to you later then, okay Lewis bye now.

Lewis walked out of the room and went back to his room, a women walked into the room and looked at Kirk.

"What are you doing in here?"

"I'm looking for some more paper for the printer and can't find it."

That's why I'm in your room, okay,

"Would you like help finding paper?"

"No," thank you, I should be just fine thanks.

Stacy quickly walked out of the room and walked on down the hall. Kirk just opened up one of the folders that was on his desk, on it, it said urgent. Kirk thought to himself I better get to it, or I may lose my job.

Suddenly the phone at his desk rang. He reached over with his right hand and grabbed the phone and put it up to his left right ear and answered and said hello this Bangle law office.

A man answered and said hi my name is Darrel, I was calling to talk to Lewis, oh okay could you please let him know that Darrel called. I will thank you. I won't call you back Sir, okay bye now. Kirk slammed the phone back down into the cradle.

The fly came back and was now buzzing around his head once again. This really irritated him and slammed his arms down on his desk and this caused the one lower drawer of his desk to open.

He looked in the drawer that opened and on a white piece of paper, he couldn't clearly see what was written on it. He put on a pair of glasses and looked at it again.

It said something about a basement, he took the piece of paper and tore it up and threw it into the trash can off to his left.

He stood up and walked out of room and was headed down to Lewis office, which he was headed there Stacy came walking down the hallway and bumped into Kirk, excuse me. I'm trying to get through and you bumped into me, excuse me Kirk.

"Why are you now in a foul mood?"

"I'm not, I'm just tired of my job. Alright bye now."

Kirk approached his bosses room and slowly walked in, Lewis was sitting behind his desk taking a big bite out of a baloney sandwich and had his left hand in a bag of chips.

There was a tall glass of soda siting on the very corner of his desk, Lewis leaned back and stopped chewing and looked at Kirk.

"What's the matter?"

"I just got a call from a customer who wanted to talk to you. "

"What was his name?"

"His name was Darrel; I know who that is."

It looks like you are enjoying your lunch, yeah I am. I love to eat junk food; I especially love to eat donuts for breakfast.

"How about you?"

"No," I don't like to eat sweets and never really eat much.

"How comes your blinds are open?"

"I just wanted to let more light in my room."

"What's going on the road nearby."

"I thought you had a job to do though. Yes, I do, then why are you watching outside. I guess just for something to watch."

"Have you saw anything interesting happen out there?"

"No," I haven't

Kirk began to look out the window and saw that there was a little boy who was crossing the street.

A car came zooming from around the corner and didn't have enough time to stop and hit the little boy.

The boy went flying up straight into the air and fell back down and landed on his side.

The driver of the car didn’t even take a minute to stop and see if the boy was okay.

“We need to do something, do what?”

“I was looking out the window and little boy just got hit by a car.”

“That’s absolutely horrific, where’s the boy now?”

“He’s laying on the ground probably unconscious and has broken legs.”

I don't think we should go out there, I’m sure that an ambulance will show up soon. No, it won't, we should go out there and do something about the boy.

"Can I please go out there and help the boy?"

"Yes," you may, thanks so much. Just be careful, I'll be fine boss.

## Chapter 8: Anxiety

I'll let you help the boy for the rest of the day. Kirk ran out of the office and ran straight over to street where the boy was laying.

He saw that there was a women holding the boy in her arms and tears were running down her cheeks.

"Is that your son?"

No, it's not, but I saw the whole accident unfold. I came running out here and saved the boy.

"Did you call 911 yet?"

"Yes," I called them, and they said that they will be here in ten minutes.

"Is the boy still awake?"

"No," his both legs are broke, when he wakes up he'll have terrible pains, you can go back. I got this taken care of

"Is there anything else I can do?"

"No," there's not, the ambulance will be here soon and take him away.

He doesn't look so good. There's blood coming out of the corner of his mouth and some blood is coming out of his left ear. I don't think he is doing so good, I'm sure he'll be fine.

Then the ambulance pulled up and the EMTs came running out of the ambulance, they quickly brought over a stretcher to where the boy was. The lady was talking to the EMTs and the EMTs didn't look so happy to be talking to the women.

The woman was talking fast and the three men that were standing around her had a puzzled look on their face.

then a car came passing by and the driver kept on looking at what was happening. The one EMT turned around and looked at the driver and said there's nothing to see here, the driver then took off and wasn't seen again.

Kirk couldn't believe what had just happened. After a few minutes the EMTs got the boy up on the stretcher and put him in the ambulance.

The women opened the back door of the ambulance and got in and sat down. The ambulance quickly pulled away; Kirk felt like he had done nothing to help. With a frown face he walked back to the office.

The air outside was full of humidity and the sweat was beginning to run down the sides of his neck. He crossed his arms and entered the building once again.

He walked back to his boss's room and his boss was now just wrapping up his lunch. He had a smile on his face and had finished eating his lunch.

"How's the boy doing?"

"I don't know when I got out there, there was a woman who was holding the boy and she had called 911 already."

She wouldn't let me help; I feel so bad about it. Don't let some grumpy old women make you upset, your heart was still in the right place.

I know but I really wanted to help the boy. Don't get down, it's just not worth it too. Just brush it off and move on, I think I'll do that.

"Now get back to your desk and go on with the rest of your day?"

"What are you doing tonight after work?"

"I'm going to a friend's house and having a beer with him. That sounds good, I'm going to a hockey game tonight with my wife and son."

I hope that your teams wins tonight, I'm sure that they will. Alright then I'm going back to work.

Talk to you later Lewis, but now Kirk. Kirk had his head down and was shaking it with his arms crossed. He sat down in his comfy desk chair and leaned back and let out a big sigh. He let out a big yawn and stretched out his arms.

"The phone rang, Kirk picked it up, hello who's this?"

"Hi Sir, it's Jenny, I was calling to find out what the hours of the office were?"

"The hours are as follows, Monday through Friday nine to five and we aren't open on the weekend."

"Did you hear about the man who had fallen into a lake that was polluted with dangerous Chemicals?"

"No," I didn't

"When did that happen?"

"I don't know the exact time, but I heard that it happened an hour ago."

"Why are you telling me this?"

"I don't have anyone else to talk to."

I'm alone most of the time and wanted to tell someone about the news I had read today.

Alright, I'm sorry, but I can't talk with you long. My boss will make me hang up if he comes in, I'm only aloud to be on the phone for more ten minutes.

"Are you afraid of your boss?"

"No," but I don't want to lose my job.

My boss is always breathing down my back. Well then perhaps you should look around for another job. I’m comfortable where I'm at. Not to cut this conversation short, but now I need to go.

Have a good afternoon, bye now. Kirk slowly put the phone back in the cradle and then began to twiddle his thumbs. He thought to himself well I've been doing good today at my job.

Then the topic of beer came into his mind, he thought about what kind of beer he was going to drink that night with his buddy.

He thought on about it and thought to himself I’m thirsty for a good hoppy ale. Then his boss came walking in and had an unusual look on his face.

"How's everything going?"

"It's going good"

"Did you just get a phone call?"

"Yes," I did

"Who was it?"

"It was an older woman who was lonely and asked me what the hours were for the office."

"Did you tell her?"

"Yes," I did

"Did she ask anything else?"

"No," her name was Jenny and she told me about something that was on the news. I bet that was a boring conversation.

"No," it wasn't, she wanted to keep on talking but I didn't want to.

Sometimes that's how calls can go. The customers tell me they like how kind of a person you are.

## Chapter 9: Another Day

You know what, I'm going to let you leave work early today. I'm going to have a meeting with the owner of this company. You can't be around, while the meeting is going on.

I'm only letting you leave an hour early. I realize that, but it's okay. I know you were late today but I that doesn't bother me at this point, you're forgiven Kirk.

So now you may pack up your stuff and you can go home, I appreciate you letting me go home early.

I hope that you have a good night tonight Lewis. Kirk got up out of his comfy office chair and shook Lewis hand and walked out of his room.

Kirk waved by to Lewis and continued to walk towards the entrance of the building. Lewis yelled out,

"Are you forgetting anything?"

"No," I don't think so, oh yeah I forgot my black leather briefcase.

Lewis carefully handed the brief case over to Kirk.

Meanwhile at Kirks house, the man who had fallen into the polluted lake, was trying to run away from his captures and had to find a place to hide. He chose Kirks basement to hide in, Kirk always has his basement locked up.

There's a big lock on the door, the man grabbed a hold of the lock and was trying to break it to open it.

The man grabbed a landscaping rock and with the sharp edge of the rock he kept on slamming the rock against the lock, hoping that the lock would eventually break apart and he could gain access.

Some of the chemicals remained on his clothes began to run down his left arm and burned some of his skin off and he could not stand the pain. He kept on grimacing in pain and was going out of his mind.

His back wouldn't stop itching and his legs itched him continually. His scalp was burning, he couldn't get any relief.

He kept on scratching his head, but it didn't seem to help. Some of his hair was beginning to fall out, he couldn't stand the sight of losing his hair.

He yelled out and said I have had enough. He kept on trying to break the lock but was not successful at it.

He went to back away from the door and the man who was trying to capture him shot at him with his pistol.

The bullet missed him and struck the doorknob and caused it to fall off and the lock came off with it.

The man who was trying to get away was just a few yards away from the convict. The convict's arms were flaring all over the place, he ran into the basement and was out of breath.

He tripped over a chair and fell flat on his face. The man that was shooting at him ran around the yard trying to find the convict.

He was getting tired of looking for him and soon gave up after an hour of looking.

Now the convict was in Kirks basement and didn't care what he ruined in the basement.

He kicked the one wooden chair; the leg of the chair came off. Then he punched a hole in the dry wall.

The convict was in such a rage that all he could see was red. He couldn't calm down and kept on punching things that he could reach. He got the chills and saw that there was an old blanket full of dust.

He quickly grabbed the blanket and threw it over his legs. The blanket had a dead stink bug, in it and it fell on him.

He didn't even care, his heart was still racing from being chased. He was glad to be in Kirks basement.

He still had the chills; he took off his wet shirt and pants. He threw them onto the basement floor, he was now half naked but didn't care at all.

He began to rummage around an old stack of clothes that were in left hand side of the basement.

He didn’t like how the old clothes looked. He thought for a moment and decided to put on the old clothes anyway.

After he put the new shirt and pants on, he slumped over into the corner of the basement.

The convict saw that there was a mini fridge in the right-hand corner of the basement. He slowly walked over to it; he opened the door to the refrigerator.

He expected it to be full of beers, but there were none there. With great rage he slammed the refrigerator door almost ripping it off of its hinges.

He walked back over to the couch and slumped down on it; he rested his head on the left arm of the couch.

Something was crawling beneath him in the foam of the couch, it didn't seem to bother him at all. He sprawled out his legs and stretched out his arms, he let out a sigh and closed his eyes.

The basement door remained open. Kirk was just about ready to get into his car. He happened to look up into the sky and huge airliner flew over him.

He could smell the stinky smell of jet fuel. The jet was flying lower than regular, Kirk could tell that something had run amuck with the plane.

He took a closer look and noticed that plane was missing its tail fin. Then as the plane went into the sunset he saw that the entire rear of the plane had caught fire.

Orange flames began to engulf the whole plane. Kirk felt so bad for the people who were on the plane. He climbed into his truck and put it in drive. He was thinking about the good time that he was going to have with his friend that night.

As he backed up he saw a car that was pulling out right behind him, the driver wasn't looking where he or she was driving.

Kirk blew the horn at the driver, the driver stopped backing up and waited for Kirk to pull out.

As Kirk drove past the other person's car, the driver gave him a dirty look. He was yelling something that he couldn't make out. Kirk just shook his head and kept on driving down the road.

He thought to himself well people really haven't been nice to me today. But that's how it is sometimes, as he thought to himself.

The sky was slowly getting dark, Kirk knew that he was going to have to turn his lights on soon.

Eventually he reached his friends house, everyone was sitting outside, talking, and having a good time together sitting by a campfire. When he got out of his car, his buddy saw him and immediately walked over to him.

"What's up man?"

"Not much."

I've got plenty of food and beer if you'd like a beer, there in the cooler by my shed.

I have chicken wings, nachos, tacos, and chips. Suddenly someone set off fireworks, I can't believe how he did that so close to you. He's probably drunk and doesn't have a clue what's going on.

"Did you let your friends ride your four-Wheeler again?"

"Yes."

He'll be just fine; he hasn't crashed yet.

"Where's your girlfriend?"

"She's away on a business trip."

She'll be back in 2 weeks; I do miss her very much. She calls me every evening, and we talk for a while.

Your yard looks good, that's because my girlfriend talked me into doing some landscaping. We also planted some trees outback, that was a muddy mess.

"What did you ever do with that fruit tree?"

"I cut it down, it was the best decision I've made in a while."

I forgot to mention, that I have cigars. No, thanks I haven't smoked in a while. Let's go sit outback on my new chairs, then you won't be around your friends.

My friend from Nebraska was supposed to come today, but so far he hasn't showed. I found these chairs to be very comfortable, they're nice.

I see that you still haven't got rid of that stump in yard, we're getting to that. My girlfriend asks me the same thing, I tell her I'll get rid of it, but I forget.

"How many acres do you have?"

"15."

I do hunt on my land, there are some nice bucks back there. We just put in some solar lights around here, I think I'm going to do that too.

"Where are you going?"

"I'm going to get you and I some wings."

While he was inside, Kirk heard a disturbance in the woods. He walked over to the patio and picked up a flashlight.

As he walked towards the woods, something in his head told him don't go in there.

He shined the flashlight into the woods and the noise stopped, it began to flicker and went out. He shook it and hit it and still nothing.

He walked a step closer to the woods and fog began to roll in. He found this to be odd, chills went down his spine. He now found himself, further into the woods.

He could hear that something was moving through the brush. The fog was settling in around him; he could hear someone whispering.

Just stop the whispering and come out and talk to me, there was no answer. Hello this isn't funny anymore, show yourself. I'm wondering who put you up to this, then a figure appeared. It was wearing all black with a hoodie over its head holding a sickle with blood dripping off of it.

Suddenly it put its skeleton hand on his shoulder and whispered in his ear. Your death is coming soon.

"What's your name?"

"My name is Reaper."

"So, you're the grim Reaper then?"

"Yes."

I'm not from your world, I'm just here to kill. I don't want to die though, every six months I come to your world to harvest the souls of my victims. I have to kill many to stay living, is very afraid of me.

When the time is right I'm going to harvest his soul. Then another figure appeared, I hope there's not two of you. I harvested his soul just today, he's a Reaper in training.

He's skin and bones just like you, but he's not as evil as I am. I was once a man just like you, and the devil came to me asking me to do his work for him.

At first I didn't comply to him, I told him to go away and to leave me alone. He left me alone for a week, then came back after me.

He appeared in my bedroom and tried to take my soul out of my body. I even shot my gun at him, this only made things worse for me.

I had a cross around my neck, this seemed to weaken him. Then somehow he called in other demons, they quickly cut my throat and I bled to death.

The coroner said that I was murdered, there was a funeral held for me. I've reaped millions of souls, and I'm going to continue.

I even reap the souls of animals, no one can ever stop me. Your soul isn’t ready for reaping yet, you're just bothering me. The blood dripping off my sickle is from an animal, I don't care to disclose what kind it was.

I thought that the Grim Reaper drank blood from his victims. Tonight, your friend will lose his life, don't interfere with my plan or I’ll haunt you every night of your life.

Many have tried to send me back to Hell using their Christian powers to stop me, but I still reaped their weak souls. The devil lives deeply underground under the capital.

Demons surround him wherever he goes, he takes children’s souls. The people that work in the buildings above the devil's throne, secretly worship him every night.

They create laws that are created with the help of demons. That sounds like a great conspiracy to me, I'm not so sure about that.

I don't care what you believe, or your feelings. I'm here to scare people to death, that's because you look so horrifying.

I've been living for hundreds of years now; the devil has thousands of reapers who work for him.

"Have you met with any of them?"

"Yes," and some of them don't even talk to their victims like I do.

They told me that I can't have a personality, I didn't believe them. When children see me they run away, or just cry out. Only the devil himself can put us to rest, I can believe that.

"Does the devil teach you about curses?"

"Yes."

Some people I've come across were somehow transitioning themselves into demons. It doesn't happen all the time though, I'll have to ask the devil.

"Did you know that the devil was once an Angel?"

"Yes"

His name was Lucifer but was shot down.

"Can you be at more than one place at a time?"

"Yes"

"How come you keep that hood over your head?"

"To keep me shielded from the light."

Here's a joke for you, I don't care about no joke. I have killed comedians before, they got on my nerves trying to make me laugh. Since I'm dead, I seem to have lost my sense of humor.

Sometimes I find my victims in cornfields plowing up the land, recently I've been having ravens following me. I don't like when they come with me because they alert my victims.

Three of them will rest on my arms, and one on my head. I try to chase them off, I've killed some of them with my sickle.

"Did you bring any of them back to life?"

"Yes," I have.

It's my only demon bird, it awaits me in my lair. Your friend is living on cursed lands, he knows about it.

The owner on the land told him after he bought the land about the land being cursed. I know who cursed the land, but he disappeared.

"Do you have any idea where he's at?"

"No."

There are plenty of satanic realms he could have gone into.

"How many of those realms are there?"

"More than I can count."

I never thought that a skeleton could count, now you know that they can. Suddenly nearby, the ground began to rise up.

It was a massive beast with four horns, three arms and two legs with glowing red eyes.

It had tusks coming out of the mouth, with large teeth. This is just one of the beasts that live on this land.

"How many of them live on this land?"

"20 of them."

I can summon them all at once if I want, but I'm not going to do that this time. If we weren't so deep in the woods, we would have crashed your friends party. These beasts were created a long time ago and live on until they're no longer needed by Satan. A war between good and evil is going to happen in just a month.

Satan is planning a massive attack on Arch Angel Michael. I don't know who that is, it's the Angel in charge of protecting the Heavens from us.

"Have you ever fought with Michael?"

"No," or I wouldn't be here.

He cuts through the demons with his special sword, no demon can withstand a blow from the sword not even the strongest.

Satan has tried many times to overwhelm him with demons to fight off, but he always kill them all. Satan says that he has the strength of 10 men.

If Satan gets killed, then we all die along with him. Your beast is waiting for you, I'm sure you want him to do something.

I want him to dig up some artifacts for me. He doesn't speak in your language, allow me to speak to him. Mox tox lox, mio misop humla huma.

I just said to him to dig up an artifact that he's familiar with. He knows several different kinds of artifacts, and where to find them.

You have wasted enough of my time, go back, and talk to your friend. I honestly thought that you were going to cut me up into pieces and curse me. I’m afraid to turn my back to you, I'm not going to do anything to you. He walked out of the woods and noticed that everyone went inside.

He opened the door and entered; someone was sitting on the floor with a beer in their hand.

He just smiled at them and continued looking for his friend, after looking in each room he went outback.

His friend was sitting down talking to a woman, he let them stew for a bit. I’m sorry bro I didn’t see you there.

Then the woman sat on his lap, while smiling at him. I can't believe that you're doing this, I’m not doing anything wrong.

“What do you call this then?”

"He unwillingly answered this isn't anything serious."

The woman got off his lap and walked away, him and Kirk walked together to a more private area. I'm having an affair with her; she works at the Bach sandwich shop downtown.

I go there to get sandwiches almost every day. Just her looks alone made me interested and her carefree attitude. She's such a flirt with me, I enjoy every minute of it.

"How old is she?"

"32."

I thought that you were done having affairs, you've been making the wrong decisions and spending time with the wrong crowd. Women just smile at you and your asking for there number.

You have a good wife and your still playing with others. Your just going to lose your wife.

I doubt your taking me serious right now, your wife will eventually catch you cheating on her.

You're probably thinking about sneaking into the bedroom and playing with her. You'll have a rude awakening one of these days.

Tell her you can't be seeing her anymore; you don't need to divulge everything. Then she'll just move on and play around with another guy she meets.

Inviting her to the party was a very bad idea. You don't seem to know how to love yourself, you rely on others to make you happy. You won't know what to do the minute she leaves you.

Your wife is probably thinking about you, and you aren't even thinking of her. You tell her you love her, but your lying to her.

You don't want to go through a divorce, so change or else. It's not that easy for me, I don't want to hear any more of your excuses. I paid off her student debt, and I'm leasing a brand-new car for her.

You’re getting yourself in deep, I’m sure your now carrying around debt. You need to seriously wake up to what’s going on around you.

You're asleep at the wheel about to crash and think nothing of it. You keep on sinning with her, you’ll be no better than the devil himself.

Your sin will be the one thing that does you in. If this continues we’ll have to end our friendship, but we have been friends for 7 years I don’t care.

You’re doing what the devil wants and you need to free yourself, from the constant evil your doing. You won’t grow spiritually if you don’t put in the effort.

Right now, you're allowing the devil to live in you. I'm not saying that women are evil, it's just you need to stop being a swinger and stop the sex, then you'll find yourself.

I have a low self-esteem, from being bullied at my job. Then speak up and tell the bully to leave you alone.

Stand up for yourself, tell yourself I'm handsome several times then say I'm a success when you wake up in the morning.

That's all I'm going to tell you, thanks for the hospitality but I better get home. They hugged one another then he left. 20 minutes later he gets a text, you're under attack by zombies.

They're coming out of the woods; I have called the police and they said they're on their way.

The zombies have already broken into my house, I'm currently sitting on my roof. My friends barely escaped them; they took off in their cars. My girlfriend is sitting beside me, that was the last text that he got from him.

When the police got there, zombies were all over the place. They fired upon several of them, this only seemed to slow them down, but they kept walking forward.

The Reaper had placed a zombie spell on the land, now the hundreds of dead where waking up. After a while the police were overrun by them, they got bitten and we're now zombies themselves.

The situation soon became an emergency, National Guard troops entered the area and began blowing up the zombies with grenades. The Reaper didn't return to murder his friend. Meanwhile up above in heaven, Michael was fighting demons and beasts. Now the Reaper, and all the evil demons were on their way to the gates of Heaven.

Michael appeared there, the Reaper said to him you're a weak Angel and I'm not afraid of you.

He said to them you'll be defeated. Michael attacked them, they fought back. With the help of the Holy Spirit, he was able to defeat them after some fierce fighting.

After the Reaper was slayed the zombie curse ended and everything went back to normal.

His friend stopped his affair and changed his outlook on things. Him and his wife, went on a cruise together that fall. Kirk went on to study psychology at the local college.

www.ingramcontent.com/pod-product-compliance
Lightning Source LLC
LaVergne TN
LVHW050314160826
845677LV00014B/3386
* 9 7 9 8 8 3 7 1 6 4 3 1 6 *